MISS SALLY ANN AND THE PANTHER

Retold by Bobbi Miller

Illustrated by Megan Lloyd

Holiday House / New York

Sources

Crockett, Davy. *The Adventures of Davy Crockett, Told Mostly By Himself.* New York: Charles Scribner's Sons, 1934.

Derr, Mark. *The Frontiersman: The Real Life and Many Legends of Davy Crockett.* New York: William Morrow & Co., Inc., 1993.

Text copyright © 2012 by Bobbi Miller

Illustrations copyright © 2012 by Megan Lloyd

All Rights Reserved

HOLIDAY HOUSE is registered in the U.S. Patent and Trademark Office.

Printed and Bound in March 2012 at Kwong Fat Offset Printing Co., Ltd.,

Dongguan City, China.

The artwork was created with acrylic paint.

The text typeface is Grit Primer.

www.holidayhouse.com

First Edition

1 3 5 7 9 10 8 6 4 2

Library of Congress Cataloging-in-Publication Data

Miller, Bobbi.

Miss Sally Ann and the panther / retold by Bobbi Miller ; illustrated by Megan Lloyd. — 1st ed.

p. cm.

Summary: Miss Sally Ann Thunder Ann Whirlwind and Fireyes the panther engage in

an epic wrestling match before becoming "great and glorious" friends.

ISBN 978-0-8234-1833-6 (hardcover)

1. Crockett, Sally Ann Thunder Ann Whirlwind—Legends. [1. Crockett, Sally Ann Thunder Ann Whirlwind—Legends.

2. Folklore—United States. 3. Tall tales.] I. Lloyd, Megan, ill. II. Title.

PZ8.1.M6122Mi 2012

398.2—dc22

[E]

2011007365

To friend Alice, great and glorious;
and to sisters of my heart
Jo D. and Susi G. Thank you.
—B. M.

For Janie, who could go nose to nose
with a panther any day!
Love, M. L.

Miss Sally Ann Thunder Ann Whirlwind
was a woman of wonder. All in a day's work,
she roped a hurricane, tied it to her spinning
wheel, and outspun the steam mill.

Then with one hand she knitted a shawl.
With her other hand she milked the cow, churned
the butter, and then baked buttermilk bread.

Come late at night, she blew out the moonlight in
a single breath and sang the wolves to sleep.

It's a fact that she had her fair share of adventures. But her finest adventure, so she told me, was her meeting Fireeyes. It happened one fine morning. It was bone-chilly, so Miss Sally Ann wore her best bear fur to the wild woods to gather onions for her stew. She came to a place where the trees grew so tall, they blocked out the sun.

Atop
the highest
branch crouched
the most savage beast:
a panther whose eyes glared
with fire. Fireeyes the panther,
five barrels long whisker to
tail, was hugeceously smart
and mean as tarnation.
Looking down at the dear
woman, he licked his
chops and twitched his
whiskers. Slowly, he lifted
his haunches in a great
swaggerous stretch. He
sharpened his claws, one at
a time, on the tree branch.

In a single bound he jumped from that limb to face
Miss Sally Ann eye to eye. His tail slithered in the air
like a snake.

Now Fireeyes thought, What a fine sleek coat that is!
That would keep my aching shoulders warm at night!

Now Miss Sally Ann thought, What a fine sleek coat
that is! That would keep my aching feet warm at night!

With a roar, the panther thrashed his tail about,
knocking down a line of oaks.

Miss Sally Ann grabbed that varmint's tail.

His mighty claws dug out a giant gorge.

Then she slung him up in the air. He flew so high and wide, she thought him lost forever.

Nope. That varmint fell like a
star. Cat that he was, he landed on his
feet, right in the middle of a briar patch.
Pricklier than ever, Fireeyes let loose a roar
so thunderific, skunks lost their stripes.

He pounced. The two tumbled backward in a scurry of petticoat and fur.

Through the day they wrestled. The panther twisted as Miss Sally Ann turned. He chomped his powerful teeth so close, she smelled his fishy breath. But she was determined to have that pelt.

She jumped on the varmint's back, grabbing
hold knuckle-white tight. He raced around and around
like a spinning top. Miss Sally Ann laughed and still kept hold.

He bounced and bounced high, past a sleeping she-eagle. Miss Sally Ann gathered eggs for her favorite eagle eggnog and still kept hold.

In one terrifiacious moment, Fireeyes reared like a mustang. The two sprawled backward. The fight turned into a true conbobberation.

Miss Sally Ann twisted as the panther turned. That varmint jumped on Miss Sally Ann's back, determined to have that coat.

Through the night they wrestled. They raised such a thunderferous racket, stars flew away like meteors. The moon dipped onto its side. The Milky Way curdled. But neither one backed down, backed up, or backed out.

By morning light Miss Sally Ann thought, Now, this panther
is a ripsnorting fine fighter.

Fireeyes thought, Now, this woman is a ripsnorting fine fighter.

For a moment they stood nose to whisker.

Then, in a twinkle, Miss Sally Ann smiled.
Sure enough, Fireeyes smiled right back at her.
And don't you know, the two became great and
glorious friends. Miss Sally Ann pulled the thorns
from the big cat's paw.

Then, lighting the way out
of the dark woods with the fire
in his eyes, Fireeyes carried the
basket of onions and eagle's eggs.

He came to be quite a handy dandy cat. He used his claws to plow the kitchen garden and used his tail to brush the chimney clean.

At night, after she blew out the moonlight, Miss Sally Ann sat by the firelight sipping her favorite eggnog. Fireeyes curled up close by to keep her aching feet warm. Miss Sally Ann covered his aching shoulders with her best bear fur.

And then, as great and glorious friends do, Miss Sally Ann
Thunder Ann Whirlwind and Fireeyes sang the wolves to sleep.